Okay Kevin

A Story to Help Children Discover How Everyone Learns Differently

James Dillon

Illustrated by Kara McHale

Jessica Kingsley Publishers
London and Philadelphia

Kevin never smiled at school.

He didn't talk much either.

But he was different at home.

He jumped up and down and did a little dance when his favorite football team scored a touchdown.

Cannonball!

He screamed, "Cannonball!" when he jumped into a swimming pool and made a big splash.

He used pretend voices for his imaginary characters when he played with blocks in his bedroom.

On his first day in kindergarten, his teacher, Mrs. Brooks, read a book about the first day of school to the class. After reading a few pages, she asked, "Who can tell me why the boy was nervous?"

As Kevin began to think of an answer, he saw five waving hands shoot up around him.

Mrs. Brooks pointed to a girl with curly brown hair wearing a yellow shirt with a rainbow across the front of it, and said, "Emma, what do you think?" Putting her hand down and taking a deep breath, Emma smiled and said, "He was worried that he might make a mistake."

Mrs. Brooks nodded and said, "Good thinking, let's read more and find out what happens."

Kevin bit down on his lower lip and thought, "That was my answer. I'll try to be faster next time."

WELCOME CLASS

Mrs. Brooks

Kevin tried harder for a lot of days and a lot of questions, but the other kids kept putting their hands up even faster, sometimes even before Mrs. Brooks had finished saying the whole question.

Kevin started to feel that he would never catch up with the other kids, no matter how hard he tried.

At night, Kevin would lie in his bed trying to figure out why school was easy for the other kids and hard for him. One night he thought, "The other kids are just faster and smarter than me. They are okay and I'm not okay."

Kevin didn't like being not okay.

One day, Mrs. Brooks said to the class, "Boys and girls, I will be meeting with each of you to find out how much you have learned. You just need to try your best."

Mrs. Brooks called each student over to a little table in the corner of the room.

Kevin watched Emma go over and sit next to Mrs. Brooks. After just a minute, Emma popped up and went back to be with the rest of the class. The same thing happened with Travis, Emily, Jamal, and the other kids.

Then it was Kevin's turn. He walked slowly over to Mrs. Brooks, who was smiling at him. She said, "Kevin, I have a list of the letters of the alphabet. I want you to say the letter that I point to." He replied, "Okay, I'll try."

Kevin looked at the letters Mrs. Brooks pointed to. He remembered some, like A, B, C, and K, right away. He had to think for a few seconds for letters like R, M, and F, and couldn't remember other letters like Q, U, G, and L.

Mrs. Brooks said to him, "Good job! Kevin, you know a lot of letters and we'll help you learn the rest. Keep trying your best. Okay?"

Kevin nodded and said, "Okay," but he was thinking that the other kids sat down and got up a lot faster than he did.

One day, his mother knocked on his bedroom door and said, "Kevin, we need to talk. I met with Mrs. Brooks and she told me that you are learning a lot and always trying your best. That's very important! But you need extra help, so you can read on grade level."

Kevin asked, "What does grade level mean?"

His mother replied, "That means that you are behind where you need to be. The other kids are learning to read a little faster than you are. With extra help you can catch up. You'll work with Mrs. Martinez, the reading teacher, every day in the reading room. Keep trying your best and everything will be okay. Okay?"

Kevin said, "Okay," but to him the words "behind" and "catch up" meant that the other kids were okay and he was not okay.

Kevin went to the reading room every day. He loved working with Mrs. Martinez and she looked like his grandmother, too. She helped him get better at reading.

Kevin kept trying his best for the rest of kindergarten, for first grade, and second grade. Even though he learned a lot, he was not reading on grade level, so Kevin still kept thinking that he was not okay.

On his first day in third grade, when he went to the reading room, Mrs. Martinez said, "Kevin, I am very excited. We are going to start a school store right here in the reading room. It will be open for the first fifteen minutes of the day. I need a store manager and I know someone who will be perfect for the job."

Kevin asked, "Who?"

Mrs. Martinez smiled and said, "You."

Kevin felt his face get warm. He had never been asked to do anything like this so he was a little nervous and excited.

Kevin asked, "Where will it be?"

Mrs. Martinez pointed to a closet door that had always been closed and said, "Let's open it and take a look. I have some school supplies and a cash register ready to go. I will teach you what you need to know." Mrs. Martinez took her key and unlocked the door.

Kevin saw shelves filled with boxes of red and white striped pencils, folders with pictures of superheroes and cartoons, erasers of different sizes and shapes, red, green, blue, and yellow notepads, and water bottles with football team logos.

Mrs. Martinez taught him how to keep track of each item that was sold, to use the catalogs to order new items, and to greet each customer with a friendly voice.

Kevin learned to make change in his head without having to write numbers down on paper. At first it was hard to do, but it got easier the more he practiced.

Mrs. Martinez pretended she was a customer and would ask Kevin for notepads and pencils and other items. She would give him different amounts of money and Kevin would make the correct change.

After practicing for many days, she said, "Kevin, looks to me like we are ready to open for business. Are we okay to go?"

Kevin replied, "Okay to go."

At first, only students stopped by, but after a few days, some teachers did, too. Kevin politely welcomed all customers, and gave them the correct change. He also never forgot to thank them for shopping at the school store.

Then one morning, as Kevin was straightening the boxes of pencils on a shelf, he heard a light knocking on the door. He turned around and saw Mrs. Polanco, the principal, standing there wearing a dark blue suit with a pair of glasses on a chain hanging down from her neck.

She said, "Hi, Kevin! I've heard that you have been doing a great job as store manager. I wonder if you could help me out."

Kevin felt his face getting a little warm and said, "Okay. What do you need?"

"I need a notepad I can fit in here," she said, as she patted the side pocket on her jacket.

"I also need two pencils in our school colors and an eraser... You know, I still make a lot of mistakes," she said, winking her eye.

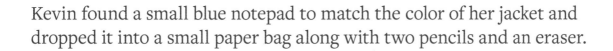

Kevin found a small blue notepad to match the color of her jacket and dropped it into a small paper bag along with two pencils and an eraser.

"That will be $2.75 please," he said in a polite voice.

Mrs. Polanco replied, "Pretty good deal!" and handed him a $5 bill.

Kevin quickly reached into the cash register, took out a quarter and two $1 bills, and gave them to Mrs. Polanco.

Laughing a little, she said, "Wow! Not only do I get a matching colored notepad for my jacket, but you also gave me the correct the change in a flash. Your brain is like a high-speed computer!"

Before Kevin could thank her, Mrs. Polanco heard her cell phone buzz and said, "Okay Kevin! I've got to go. Thanks for your help!" And she was gone down the hallway.

As he sat behind the cash register, Kevin pictured his brain as a computer and thought that maybe he wasn't so slow after all.

Later, as Kevin walked to his classroom, he could still hear Mrs. Polanco's voice saying two words over and over again in his head, "Okay Kevin. Okay Kevin."

He whispered softly to himself, "If Mrs. Polanco thinks I am okay, maybe I really might be okay."

Later that day, when Kevin was going down the hall to the reading room, he saw Mrs. Polanco coming out of her office holding the blue notepad in one hand.

She stopped, looked at him, and smiled. Then, with her other hand, she put her pointer finger on the tip of her thumb, spread the other three fingers apart, and moved them slightly toward him.

Kevin just nodded back, but wasn't sure what Mrs. Polanco was trying to tell him.

Principal's Office

reading room

Later, at home, Kevin told his mother about his day at school. "Mom, I sold Mrs. Polanco a notepad, pencils, and an eraser. I gave her the right change and she told me that I had a brain like a fast computer."

"That's great, Kevin," his mom replied.

"Then later I saw Mrs. Polanco in the hallway and she did this." Kevin put his pointer finger on the tip of his thumb and spread his other three fingers apart.

"What does it mean?" he asked.

His mother answered, "That's the okay sign, Kevin. Mrs. Polanco is telling you that you did a good job. You helped her. No surprise to me. You are a great helper!"

His mother made the okay sign and Kevin did too.

Giving him a big hug, his mother said, "Kevin, I have an idea! Whenever you feel nervous or scared about anything that's hard to do at school, you can make the okay sign to yourself. It will calm you down so you can do your best. What do you think?"

Kevin said, "Okay. I'll try it."

And he did, every day at school.

When Kevin was reading and saw a word he didn't know right away, he took a deep breath, made the okay sign, and figured it out the way Mrs. Martinez taught him.

The okay sign became his secret weapon against hard words and questions. The more Kevin used it, the more words became easier for him to read. Books became easier to read too, even chapter books.

Kevin kept working as the school store manager and got to know almost everybody in the school, even fifth graders and the teachers.

They would sometimes ask him, "How do you make change in your head so fast?"

Kevin answered, "When you do something a lot, you get better. Just keep trying, even if it's hard."

So when third grade was almost over, Kevin had forgotten about catching up to the other kids.

Then one day, Kevin heard a light knocking on the school store door. He looked up and saw Mrs. Polanco standing there in the same blue suit with the same pair of glasses hanging down from her neck.

"Hey, Kevin! Guess what? I need two more notepads this time. The pencils and the eraser are still working okay for me," she said.

Kevin found two blue notepads to match her suit and put them in a small bag, saying, "That will be $1.50, please."

Mrs. Polanco reached into her pocket and pulled out a $10 bill. She looked at it and said, "Uh oh, that's all I have. Can you make change?"

Kevin quickly reached into the cash register and pulled out a $5 bill, three $1 dollar bills, and two quarters, and handed them to her along with the paper bag.

"Wow, faster than ever. What service too! Thanks again," she said, shaking her head in amazement.

She glanced at the clock on the wall and said, "Okay Kevin. I've got to go."

As she was heading out the door she heard Kevin's voice. "Excuse me! Mrs. P, you forgot something!"

Turning around, Mrs. Polanco mumbled, "Huh, what did I...?" but stopped when she saw Kevin standing there showing her the okay sign.

"You forgot to let me thank you for shopping at the school store. Thanks," Kevin declared.

Mrs. Polanco smiled and said, "Oh, I guess I forgot something too."

She took a pen from her inside jacket pocket and a notepad from her bag. Putting her glasses on and bending over the desk, she wrote something in the notepad and then carefully removed that page from it.

"Here," she said, handing it to Kevin. "Read it out loud, please."

Kevin looked at the note and read it in a loud and clear voice:

Dear Kevin,

Thanks for your help!

You do a great job as the school store manager and as a student!

You are A #1 OKAY in my book.

Keep up the good work!

Your friend,
Mrs. Polanco

"Kevin, don't ever forget that. Okay?"

Kevin nodded and said, "Okay. I won't."

"Good. Gotta go," she said and left in a flash.

Kevin read the note silently to himself five times and then looked at the clock. It was time to close the store. He shut the door behind him, walked over to Mrs. Martinez, and handed her the note from Mrs. Polanco.

Mrs. Martinez read the note, handed it back to him and said, "I agree, 100%!"

Kevin took the note, placed it in the chapter book he was reading, and said, "I'll use it as my bookmark. Okay?"

Mrs. Martinez nodded and replied, "Okay Kevin."

Nodding back, Kevin said, "See you later, Mrs. Martinez. Gotta go!"

Then, tucking the book under his arm, he twirled around, did a little skip, and strode out of the reading room.

As Kevin walked down the hallway to his classroom, the smile on his face grew bigger with every step he took.

A Guide for Parents and Educators

Kevin's story provides a springboard for talking to children about learning in school. His story can help them reflect on their experiences in school and explore their feelings about their learning in relation to their peers. By understanding the concept of learning, children will avoid interpreting the variation in speed of acquiring skills as a sign that something is wrong with them – that they are not "okay."

Kevin's story can help them reflect on and explore their own talents and abilities. The key message of Kevin's story is that all children are capable and have something valuable to contribute to their school community.

Here are some things to talk about with children regarding learning:

Learning takes time and is not a competition. Parents and educators can share their own learning stories with children. Children see adults performing a variety of skills automatically and mistakenly assume these skills were easily acquired. Children benefit from the back stories of how adults often struggled with learning things they now perform routinely. Adults can share how they felt frustrated when first learning to ride a bicycle or tie shoes. Unless children can hear how frustration and initial difficulty turned into success, they can feel their frustration will never end.

→ Why did Kevin feel like he couldn't catch up to the other students?
→ Why did Kevin think that getting help for reading meant he was not "okay"?
→ Why did Kevin start to think he was "okay" after he started working in the school store?

Everyone learns different things in different ways. Since the school experience highlights the importance of academic learning, primarily in language arts and mathematics, children can underestimate their abilities in other areas, such as music, art, athletics, and interpersonal skills. Children need opportunities to discover the different aptitudes they might have in non-academic domains. In addition, they need adult guidance to help them understand how a community benefits from a diversity of skills and abilities from different people.

→ How did Mrs. Polanco help Kevin start to feel he was "okay"?
→ Why did Kevin improve his reading skills after he started working in the school store?
→ Why was it important for Kevin to know that he was helping his school?

People can develop strategies for coping with difficult or challenging tasks. Being prepared for difficulties and challenges is the best way for emotionally dealing with them. Children can inadvertently think learning *should* occur easily and can be overly attuned to even the slightest difficulty or challenge. Having a simple plan that has been practiced ahead of time can help children recognize their feelings and guide them past an initial reaction of helplessness. Such a plan can be a simple "If...then" routine a child can learn, for example, "If I don't know the answer right away, then I can take a deep breath."

→ How did the "okay" sign help Kevin read difficult words?
→ How did the "okay" sign give Kevin confidence for reading?
→ What other signs or strategies could Kevin have used?

Problems are opportunities for learning. Our culture sometimes conveys the message that mistakes or problems either shouldn't happen or that they should immediately be corrected or fixed. In reality, however, problems and mistakes are how we learn and grow. In addition, the emotion of encountering new problems or mistakes can easily erase the memory of past successes of solving problems and learning from mistakes. Some children benefit from keeping a written record of these successes to develop confidence in themselves as learners. Children who have learned to reframe difficulties and hardships as opportunities develop a resilience they can rely on for the rest of their lives.

→ How did Kevin's feelings change from the beginning of the story to the end?
→ What do you think would have happened if Kevin had never had the chance to work in the school store?
→ Why was the note from Mrs. Polanco so important to Kevin?
→ Compare your story of school to Kevin's. How is it the same? How is it different?

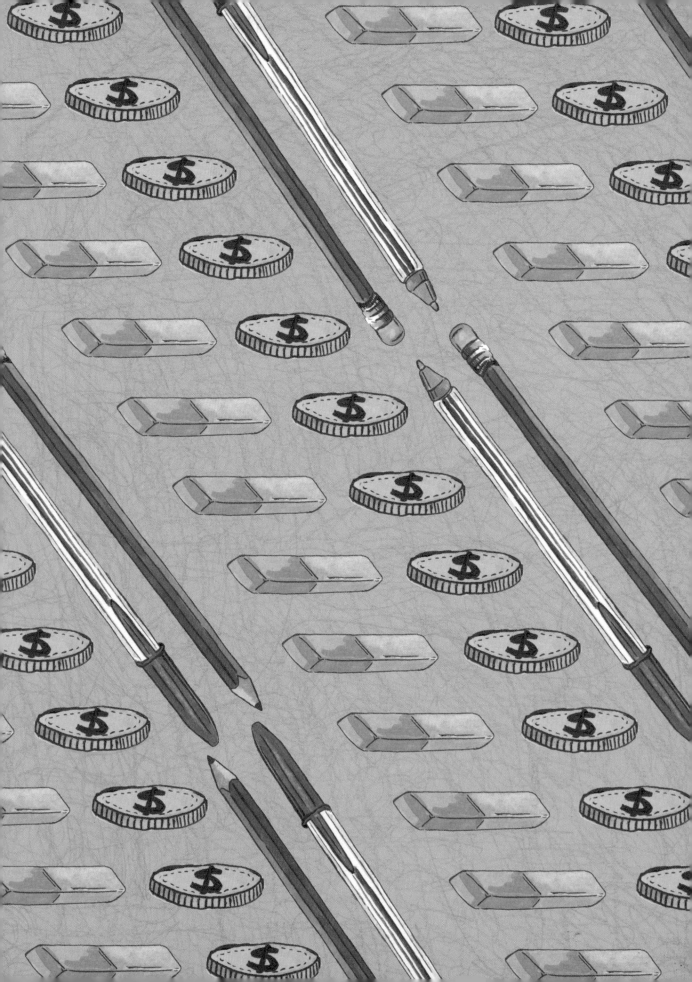